Dear Parent:

Your child's love of reading starts here!

Every child learns to read in a different way and at his or her own speed. You can help your young reader improve and become more confident by encouraging his or her own interests and abilities. You can also guide your child's spiritual development by reading stories with biblical values and Bible stories, like I Can Read! books published by Zonderkidz. From books your child reads with you to the first books he or she reads alone, there are I Can Read! books for every stage of reading:

SHARED READING
Basic language, word repetition, and whimsical illustrations, ideal for sharing with your emergent reader.

BEGINNING READING
Short sentences, familiar words, and simple concepts for children eager to read on their own.

READING WITH HELP
Engaging stories, longer sentences, and language play for developing readers.

READING ALONE
Complex plots, challenging vocabulary, and high-interest topics for the independent reader.

ADVANCED READING
Short paragraphs, chapters, and exciting themes for the perfect bridge to chapter books.

I Can Read! books have introduced children to the joy of reading since 1957. Featuring award-winning authors and illustrators and a fabulous cast of beloved characters, I Can Read! books set the standard for beginning readers.

A lifetime of discovery begins with the magical words **"I Can Read!"**

Visit www.icanread.com for information on enriching your child's reading experience.
Visit www.zonderkidz.com for more Zonderkidz I Can Read! titles.

Be kind and tender to one another.
Forgive each other, just as God forgave
you because of what Christ has done.
—*Ephesians 4:32*

To my dad, who shops like Howie.
—*S.H.*

ZONDERKIDZ

Howie Goes Shopping
Copyright © 2008 by Sara Henderson
Illustrations copyright © 2008 by Aaron Zenz

Requests for information should be addressed to:
Zonderkidz, *Grand Rapids, Michigan 49530*

Library of Congress Cataloging-in-Publication Data

Henderson, Sara, 1952-
      Howie goes shopping / story by Sara Henderson ; pictures by Aaron Zenz.
         p. cm. — (I can read! My first level)
      Summary: Howie sneaks into the car and joins Emma and her mother at the
      supermarket, makes a mess while having a wonderful time, and learns about
      forgiveness.
      ISBN: 978-0-310-71606-8 (softcover)
      [1. Shopping—Fiction. 2. Forgiveness—Fiction. 3. Dogs—Fiction. 4. Animals—
Infancy—Fiction. 5. Christian life—Fiction.] I. Zenz, Aaron, ill. II. Title.
      PZ7.H3835Hov 2008
      [E]—dc22

                                      2007034315

Editor: *Betsy Flikkema*
Art direction: *Jody Langley*
Cover design: *Sarah Molegraaf*

Printed in China

09 10 11 12 13 • 6 5 4 3 2

ZONDERkidz

I Can Read!

SHARED READING

My First

HOWIE GOES SHOPPING

story by Sara Henderson

pictures by Aaron Zenz

Where is Howie?

He is hiding in the car.

Does Mother see him?

Does Emma see him?

Mother parks at the store.

Howie jumps out.

Oh no! Howie was in the car!
Catch him, Emma!

The floor is slick.

Howie slips and slides.

Howie jumps up.

Look at him run!

Can Emma catch Howie?
Run, run, run!

There he goes.

Howie likes shopping.

Crash! Crash!

Rumble!

Splat!

People are stopping.

Apples are dropping
on the day that
Howie goes shopping.

"Stop, Howie, stop!"

There goes Howie.

Howie sees candy.

Yum, yum, shopping is fun.

Crash! Crash!

Rumble!

Splat!

People are stopping.

Candy is dropping
on the day that
Howie goes shopping.

Emma chases Howie.

Howie runs fast.

Howie sees cakes and pies.

Yum, yum, shopping is fun.

Crash!

Crash!

Rumble!

Splat!

People are stopping.

Pies are dropping
on the day that
Howie goes shopping.

Emma runs fast.

Howie runs faster.

Howie sees balloons.

Shopping is like a party.

Pop!

Pop!

Poppity-pop!

People are stopping.

Balloons are popping
on the day that
Howie goes shopping.

"Howie, stop right now!"

Howie looks at Emma.

"Howie, you made a mess.
It's a big, big mess."

"Please don't be mad
at Howie," said Emma.

"He didn't mean to make a mess," said Emma. "I will clean it up."

Everyone laughs and helps.

Howie helps too.

Howie is happy.

Emma still loves him.

Shopping is not for puppies!